by

M. A. Jagendorf

ILLUSTRATED BY

SHANE MILLER

The

Merry Men

of Gotham

THE VANGUARD PRESS, INC.

NEW YORK

To Grace & Jim
Mix

Contents

Illustrations

Hear ye!

HEAR YE! Hear Ye!! Hear Ye!!! All lasses and lads from eight to eighty. These are the silvery tales

I

of the men of Gotham and some about Jack of Dover's search for the fool of fools in England. They are merry and silly, wise and otherwise! Here they are, tumbling around you like white blossoms from an apple tree on a rosy spring day.

In olden times Gotham in England was called Goats' town because those who lived there had many grazing goats. The people of the town watched the black-and-white-haired animals and saw that they were always happy, butting playfully and full of sly tricks.

"Our town is famous for our gay goats. Let us act as they do and see if we, too, can't always be happy."

Said and done. Soon "Goats' town" was called Gotham, famous for its merry men with their sly pranks and slier wit.

They solved the hardest riddles. They wriggled out of arguments with ironclad knights to whom people were afraid to speak. They solved knotty problems in a way no one ever had before!

4

Once the men of Gotham had to act silly to stop
King John of England from stealing their land. The
King was fooled, and there was great joy.

"Ha, if it's wise to be foolish, why not act silly
more often!" they cried one and all.

From then on they played all sorts of skimble-
skamble tricks, and soon it became a habit.

The fame of the rollicking deeds of the men of
Gotham and Jack of Dover's wild-goose search spread
through all lands, and people laughed at them. For
that reason I will now tell them to you.

This is how it began

THERE was a king in England, and they called him
John. And though a king should be good and wise,

John was hard and fierce, and people feared him.

This curly-headed King John, with a train of knights and beautiful ladies in velvet and fur, rode up and down the land, and wherever the royal foot touched the earth, it became a public highway. So the King gained many roads where there had been no roads, and the citizens lost many fields where good food had grown.

One day Robert, the guzzling herald in gay colors, came to the bustling market place of Gotham. He cried that the King and his court were on their way to Oakham and would rest in Gotham. This was a warning for the citizens to make ready the finest chambers and to prepare the best meats and drink for the royal company.

The guzzling herald was a stout man with three chins under his thick lip, and the long speech made him hungry. So he went into the inn to sample the red beef and pink-brown hams that his royal master would soon be crunching.

7

The good men of Gotham did not like the icy news, and they called a council under the great shielding oak tree. There came Tol the draper and Robin the cheeseman. There were Richard and Tom, Brian and Harry; there were weavers, tanners, furriers, vintners, and husbandmen. All Gotham was there.

Spoke Richard, the red-haired alderman, "The Lord ha' mercy on us. Greedy King John and his greedy nobles will pass here, and we'll lose our good land. It's a shame!"

"If it were King Richard the Lionhearted," said John the blacksmith with the big voice, "I'd not mind it. But by hoof and anvil, it's not he!"

There were many cheers at the name of lionhearted Richard.

"Talk'll help us little," cried Dame Elizabeth.

Up rose Robin the cheeseman with the single eye. He was a long, thin, strong man, with a nose like a bird's beak and a straggly beard which hung down his leather jerkin.

8

"We are famous for our merry ways," he said, "but our merry ways will do us little good now. Why not try to act silly instead? Perhaps folly will help us where wisdom fails."

A shout went up, and all agreed it was worth a trial. Instead of being wise, they'd be foolish; instead of acting friendly, they'd be hostile; instead of being clever, they'd be silly.

The guzzling herald came from the inn. He was so full of good food and drink that he walked very slowly.

"Ho, there!" thundered Robin with the single eye. "Tell King John he can't pass through Gotham. That is our reply and order."

Added Fat Ned, "We think what we list and fear nothing."

The herald opened his mouth and goggled his eyes like a fish and did not say a word for a long time, so sick with surprise was he. Finally, he spluttered and barked:

9

"You'll pay for this, you raggy villains!" Then he mounted his steed and rode off, in greater fury than any fat man since the day of Adam.

King John was feasting and drinking when he heard the news. His anger was fierce and his order sharp.

"Send twenty knights to clear the way and the town as well. Make of it a grazing ground for goats."

The knights in cold iron and their wolfish followers rode off. Their faces were black, and their steel pikes, swords, and battle-axes gleamed sharp!

But the merry Gotham folk were ready. They had no battle-axes, no lances, no two-edged swords, no bows; they just had their wits.

The wicked crew ready for blood and butchery soon came to the road that led into Gotham—and stopped, at the strangest sight in the world.

Red Richard the alderman stood at the hurrying brook, pouring pail after pail of water into a big green tub without a bottom, which a short round man held in both his hands. The water poured out as quickly as it was poured in.

"By our Lady, fool, what are you doing?" roared the leader of the knights.

"Sir knight, I am trying to fill the tub with water," said Richard innocently. The knights howled with laughter at this.

Nearby, men had brought up a cart with sunburnt hay and were unloading it outside a barn.

"Since when is hay kept outside the barn?" cried another knight.

"That's to keep the barn in the shade," replied the Gotham citizens solemnly.

Women in red and green kirtles and barefoot children were running about with open pots and baskets.

"Why are they running around like this?" cried another knight.

"To catch sunshine to light our chambers at night," they said.

A man was walking carrying on his back a door

11

with a lock. Asked why, he replied, "To make sure my house is locked while I'm away."

Men were shouting for the flies to leave Gotham. A fellow stood on a ladder against a tree, painting green apples red. Some were trying to catch their shadows. Men and women, boys and girls, were throwing salt at birds' tails, to catch them. In short, each one was acting more silly than the next.

The knights under their steel and leather looked and laughed, not knowing what to make of it.

"They're mad! To punish them would be as silly as their deeds. They wouldn't know why they were punished!" "We'll go back to King John and tell him of this"—said one and another.

So they returned and told their tale. King John laughed and agreed that there was little use in punishing madmen.

But one thought differently—and that was sleek Jack of Dover, a big fellow going up and down the roads of England to find the greatest fool in the land.

12

"Sir knight, I am trying to fill the tub with water," said Robert innocently.

"I'm off to Gotham," he cried. "I think they are only playing the fool to gain their own ends."

"Go and find out and come back and tell me. There'll be a good reward for you if what you say is true," said King John.

Off went Jack of Dover to Gotham town, while King John and his knights went on another road, telling everywhere about the silly men of Gotham.

As for those in Gotham, they were full of joy at the trick they had played on the greedy king.

"We are the wisest people in the world," they cried, "for we are wise when we are silly. Who ever heard of such a thing!"

"Why not act silly all the time," roared John the blacksmith. "We citizens, without weapons, gained a great victory over knights in armor and steel with just good laughter. Truly, we are the merry and wise men of Gotham."

"Let us act silly and merry always, for it is to our gain and makes life easy," shouted Big Harry the vintner.

15

The seed was sown and fruit began to grow. From then on, Gotham men acted differently from anyone else, and they found that they got what they wanted much easier and that life was more merry for it.

Cuckoo in the
hedge

NOW, I'll tell you the next tale—no, I'll sing you the next tale. To tell the truth, sometimes the two are

3

the same. For a merry tale is like a sweet song. Besides, it is about a song, a madrigal of the merry men of Gotham—a cuckoo bird singing in their meadow, Jack of Dover, and the fat herald.

Sparkling spring had come to sunny England, and the green meadows and sprouting woods around Gotham town were a-thrilling.

On the yellow, dusty roads, travelers were coming and going, and among them were sleek Jack of Dover and Robert, the fat guzzling herald. Both were arguing about the men of Gotham, whether they were truly silly or not. Robert said they were; Jack said no.

"Let us go and see," they agreed. So they turned to Gotham road and came there on a Sunday. Since it was the month of May, the month of delight, all the people of Gotham—men, women, and children—had gone to make springtime joy and dance around the Maypole that stood in the middle of the town.

The rainbow birds, seeing the company and hop-

18

ing for crumbs, had joined the merriment, and none sang louder than the cuckoo, the little gamin who lays its eggs in other birds' nests.

When the dancing and singing were done and the company sat down to a grand feast, the cuckoo was still at his own music game loudly and cheerily.

"I like the song," said Joan, the alderman's daughter.

"The song is sweet, indeed," said Dame Alys, the alderman's wife.

Now, when Dame Alys and Joan said they liked the same thing, Richard the alderman was not the man to refuse it to them. Besides, other women and children now said the same.

"Oh, if I only could have the lovely cuckoo sing in winter as well as summer!" spoke young Joan again.

"I'd get it for you if I could," said Martin, the saddler's apprentice, who loved Joan.

"And why can't you?" quoth Richard the alderman. "Marry, why not? We men of Gotham who could outwit a king of the realm surely can outwit a cuckoo."

He called a council then and there, and it was decided to keep the cuckoo singing all the year 'round. This for the joy and pleasure of Joan and of all the others as well.

"Let us build a hedge around the bird," cried Martin bravely.

It was the first thought of how it was to be done, and it seemed a good one.

No sooner said than the task was begun. The men turned to cutting trees, setting them in the earth, and tying them stoutly. As for the bird, he sat on the bush, singing gayly.

It did not take long till the hedge was made all around, but there was no roof on it yet.

Right then there came to the meadow Robert the herald and Jack of Dover. First to see them was Henry the miller; he ran up to Richard the alderman.

20

"Aren't the men of Gotham the silliest of England? Those fools never thought of a roof."

"Alderman," he whispered, "the herald and Jack of Dover are here to spy on us."

"Oh, is that the game!" said Richard. "We'll fool them in our good old Gotham way. The work is now done," he cried. Then, "What do you think of our fine cuckoo hedge, Master Robert and Jack of Dover? We made it so the bird won't fly away."

Cried Tol the draper, "Sing here all the year, and thou shalt lack neither meat nor drink."

Jack and the herald looked and listened, and while they looked the bird suddenly rose in the air, over the top of the hedge, and flew away, crying loudly: "Cuckoo! Cuckoo!"

"A vengeance on her," said Richard the alderman. "We made not our hedge high enough. That was silly of us indeed. Another foot of hedge, and she would never have escaped us."

Guzzling Robert, the herald, looked at Jack of Dover.

"What did I say?" said Robert. "Aren't the men of

23

Gotham the silliest of England? Those fools never thought of a roof!"

Jack of Dover did not know what to think. He was not yet certain whether the men of Gotham were truly silly or just sly.

But to this day, not far from Gotham you can see "Cuckoo Bush Hill," where the hedge was raised to keep the bird singing all the year 'round.

Three men on the bridge

IN merry Gotham, as in the rest of the round, rolling world, all the people were not alike. Most were gay,

4

but some were like a cold, rainy autumn morning.

One day Tol the draper was on the way to Nottingham to buy sheep. He was a happy, little bird-like man, with a pointed beard and a narrow yellow face.

He reached Nottingham bridge, where he saw, coming the other way, Giles the gooseman, who resembled the birds he sold. Giles was full of black anger because he had driven a poor bargain at the fair.

"Well met," piped Tol in his chipper little voice.

"Whither go you?" growled Giles gruffly.

"Marry, friend Giles, to Nottingham market to see if I can't buy a few good sheep at a bargain price."

"And which way will you bring them home?" snorted Giles.

"Straight over this bridge, friend Giles. Come, put a smile on your face and a little cheer in your voice, or I'll not call you friend."

"Little do I care what you call me," griped Giles.

26

"But, by Robin Hood, you'll not drive your sheep over this bridge on which I stand."

He said this because he was in a harsh humor and wanted to be contrary.

"By Maid Marion," screamed Tol, "I will."

"You will not," roared Giles.

"I will," said Tol. "Neither you nor the King's knights can stop me."

"You will not. Shoo away from here, Master Tol with the face of a weasel."

"Shoo yourself from here, Master Giles with the face of a bellowing bull-calf. And don't you dare call me weasel-face," cried Tol, raising his thin stick while Giles raised his thick stick. But both were wise citizens and stood a good distance apart so that they could not strike each other. Both began beating the wind and the earth. Giles hit the road so hard that the dust flew high, while Tol swung his thin stick so hard that it whistled like a storm.

"You can't stop my sheep," shouted Tol hoarsely.

27

"They shall not come this way," bawled Giles.

"They shall."

"If you argue more, I'll stick my finger in your mouth."

"The devil you will."

"Yes, I . . ."

They might have come to real blows if good fortune had not sent their way Henry, the fat miller of Gotham. He came walking from the cool woods, while his horse followed, a sack of flour loaded upon its back.

The two stopped their argument.

Right then a fourth fellow came by. It was Jack of Dover, going to Gotham to find out if the men there were really silly or not. He stopped a ways off and looked at the three and listened. But Henry the miller had seen him and knew the game he had to play.

Said Henry slowly and loudly, "What's wrong with you two?"

Each tumbled over the other to tell about the sheep that were not there.

"Ah, fools, will you never learn wit?" said Henry after he had listened to them. "Fighting about sheep walking over a bridge when the sheep are not even bought. I'll show you how little your argument is worth. Come, both of you—but first take this sack of flour from my horse and lay it upon my shoulders."

They did as they were told.

"Now," continued Henry, "let us go to the middle of the bridge and hold the bag over the water."

The three went on the bridge.

When they got to the middle of the bridge, Henry unloosened the mouth of the sack. At once, the flour began to pour out, running into the water.

When it was empty, Henry spoke:

"Now, neighbors, Giles and Tol, tell me how much meal is there in the sack?"

"Marry," answered they, "none."

"Now, by my faith," said wise Henry, "even so

much wisdom is there in your two heads to strive and battle for the sheep which are not here."

Jack of Dover, laughing, came up and said:

"Did you say these two had no sense for fighting over nothing? I think you have less sense than they for throwing your flour away to prove it. Ha, ha, now I know I have found the greatest fools of England, but I can't make up my mind which of you is the worst."

"The worst fool is one who thinks everyone else is a fool. Remember that, Master Jack of Dover," said the stout miller.

Hearing this, Jack of Dover went his way none the wiser than he had come. He wondered whether the three men of Gotham on the bridge had acted silly or not. I bet a penny you know.

The poor ploughman and the rich nobleman

NOW, Jack of Dover was roaming up and down the
yellow, dusty roads, making his search for the fool

5

of fools and making inquiries in most of the places in England.

One day he came to Devonshire, where he found there dwelt a country ploughman who, because of his simpleness, was made a fool of by almost everyone. Most people thought he acted as silly as the merry men of Gotham.

There was also in the town a rich gentleman who, more than any other, made sport of this poor ploughman. He was a mean man, ever greedy for what others had.

Now, the poor ploughman had a fat, sleek milch cow that the gentleman had seen and wanted as his own; and, knowing what a fool the ploughman was, he figured he could get the animal without paying a copper for it.

Every time he met the simple man, he told him of the well-known good words, to wit, what whosoever gives a gift with a full good will of the heart will be

32

repaid doubly by the Lord in Heaven before the year is over.

The poor ploughman, hearing these words again and again, thought 'twould be fine to have two kine for his one cow in a year's time. So, one day when he heard the gentleman say it for perhaps the twentieth time, and seeing the great benefit to him in his poverty if he had two cows instead of one, he said:

"Your worship, take my milch cow with my good will and God's blessing, and may she return double before the year is over, as you, good sir, said 'twould happen."

The gentleman took the fat animal and led it to his meat house, where he kept his other kine.

"Ha, what a witless fool," cried he. "I knew I'd get the beast from that numskull without paying. Never will he see it again."

He smiled and rubbed his hands, well contented with his misdeed.

The poor ploughman waited patiently through the

33

changing days and moving months, hoping two cows would come back for the one he had given away.

One evening he was sitting at his bare table eating bread and milk when he heard a cow mooing at his window. He ran out quickly, and there, certain as the stars, stood his cow—with another animal, a fine fat ox, just as the good gentleman had promised and foretold.

Now, you know, cows ever have a way of wanting to return to their old home, and so this cow had come back to her old home, and the fat ox had followed her.

Of course, the poor ploughman did not think of this. He believed the Lord, through the gentleman, had rewarded him for giving away his cow with a good will.

He raised his hands in thankful prayer for the blessing and said:

"See how the Lord works with this good gentleman: for he, pitying my estate, hath sent my cow

34

And there, certain as the stars, stood his cow with a fine fat ox.

double home. Indeed, I will take this lordly gift from his hands most thankfully."

He drove both the cattle into his stall, butchered the ox at once, and salted him away in his tubs for the coming months.

The next morning he took the cow back to the gentleman and said:

"Yesternight you sent my cow back doubly, according to your word, and here I bring her back again, hoping once more for the benefit of your good courtesy"—meaning he would once again get two cows for the one.

The gentleman thought the poor ploughman was only speaking foolish words and had brought back the animal that had wandered off. He took the cow and put her in the stable with his other kine, never noting that one was gone.

But a week later the cow once again came back to her old home for exactly the same reason as before, bringing with her another ox. The poor ploughman

37

was overjoyed and thanked the Lord and the rich gentleman from his very heart. He salted away the second ox to sell the meat, and returned his own again.

This happened week after week, maybe five or six times, until the foolish ploughman had the finest beefs of the gentleman who had tried to cheat him.

Then one fine day the rich man discovered what had been going on, and he raised a hue and cry and went to the judge, dragging the ploughman along.

The judge listened, and so did many a man, among them Jack of Dover.

The judge held, and so did all who heard, that the gentleman could never recover anything at the poor man's hands because he had promised him, and did not deny it, double for his gift.

"Now, this to my mind was pretty foolery," said Jack of Dover, "but yet the fool of fools is not here found that I look for."

38

So up he rose to continue his search throughout England.

A cat may look on a king: and what of that?
When a cat so looketh, a cat is still a cat.

High diddle diddle,
the fool in the middle

THERE was a merry man of Gotham a-riding on
the road. His name was Brian, and though many

called him silly, his life was full of laughter, which the many did not have. Merry Brian was sitting high on his bony piebald, and before him lay a yellow, bulging sack filled with two bushels of good wheat. He was riding to the market, full of joy at the money he would earn. To pass the time away he hummed a song:

> Dibbity, dibbity, dibbity, doe,
> Give me a pancake and I'll go.
> Dibbity, dibbity, dibbity, ditter,
> Please give me a bit of a fritter.

This was a little song sung by young folks on Shrove Tuesday in the still dusk to get a bit of pancake or a fritter. Merry Brian hummed the verse over and over, then he laughed loudly, remembering how the song had gained him many a good mouthful.

All of a sudden a crow, flashing blue-black in the

sun, flew across his horse. That was an ill omen, so he cried:

Crow, crow, get out of my sight,
Or I'll kill your father and mother tonight.

The crow flew off, crying caw, caw, and our merry man in green fustian was once again happy as the day.

Just as he was coming near Nottingham to

Nottinghamshire Full of Hoggys

a tattered, steel-dark cloud passed across the sun, and the sun and the face of good Brian darkened.

"Alas," cried he, "I'm no better than a wild beast in the weird woods. Here I am sitting in great comfort atop o' my faithful horse that's labored for me many a year, and on top o' that I'm burdening the poor, kind beast, that has served me well, with two

42

bushels of wheat on its back. Fie! I'm the cruelest carl in all of England."

Every moment he grew more angry at the thought. "Shame upon me! Of what degree man am I to act so like a churl? I must have but half a heart."

He came to a brown wooden bridge spanning a little sparkling river, stopped the horse, and got down from it. Next he took off the sack full of wheat and put it across his own neck and tried to climb on the horse, but it was not easy. As luck would have it, Jack of Dover came by right then. Brian knew him well.

"Come, Jack," he cried, "help me mount my horse."

"Why don't you put the sack on the horse and then get up?" queried Jack.

"Because, friend Jack, I don't want to burden my good horse with the load of wheat. 'Tis sufficient that he carries me without complaint. I'll carry the wheat upon my back and save my good animal."

Jack looked and listened and did not know what to

43

say. He was not certain whether Brian had played a game to fool him or was acting silly naturally. But he helped him get on the horse. Brian thanked him and went off with a light heart and a heavy burden on his neck.

"Friend," cried he to the horse, swallowing hard, "thus I reward you for your many years of service. By cock and fox, the burden is no longer upon your back but upon my neck."

But Brian never felt the burden at all, for a good deed drives weight or worry away.

So he rode along in the sparkling sun, gay as any flashing bird in the air, while Jack of Dover still stood there like a plucked crow, greatly worried whether Brian was a fool or had done the silly thing just to fool him.

Now won't you sing with me:

High diddle diddle,
The fool in the middle.

Raking for the moon

GRACE, the sweet daughter of Robin the cheese-man, was in love with young Arthur, the glover's apprentice. Now, Robin, who was rich in gold but poor in brains, wanted his daughter to marry a fat old tanner in Nottingham. For that reason he watched over the lovely girl as over a prisoner, and she could never see her sweetheart. Truly, Robin was a silly man.

The Midsummer Eve festival came, and all the town went forth to the green to make merry.

But not once could Grace and Arthur speak to each other alone or walk together as other boys and girls did. This made them both unhappy.

The big yellow moon shone in the sky, and in the quiet river that ran through the soft meadow there was a true copy of it. In the water it looked yellowish, like the big cheeses made in that part of England.

Arthur walked under the trees heavy with warm green leaves till he reached the river. He looked at the yellow moon in the dark-blue sky and saw how it also shimmered in the gleaming water as the bullfrogs croaked and croaked their deep evening song. All of a sudden it gave him an idea. . . .

46

He walked back and found Grace's mother and father.

"Master Robin," said he, "I think there is a big yellow cheese lying in the river that flows in your meadow."

"What! A cheese in the river!" cried Robin. "I must get it," and he ran as quickly as his legs would carry him to see it. His wife and others followed.

"Now," whispered Arthur to Grace, "you and I can walk together," and he took her hand, and they went off.

Many people understood the young fellow's scheme. They liked him and saw no harm in it, so they just smiled and kept silent.

Jack of Dover was present, too. He was forever haunting Gotham's homes and inns and meadows and fields to learn if the people there were truly silly or playing a game to fool the ruler of the land. For King John had promised Jack gold and honors if he but caught the men of Gotham mocking him. But the

47

alderman and many of the townspeople were ever on the watch.

Rich Robin came to the shimmering river and saw the image of the round yellow moon in it. It really did look like a fine, big cheese.

"Here's a bit of good luck!" he cried. "This good cheese is in the river on my land and so belongs to me. But this is a day of feasting, so when I fetch it each one will get a good slice."

Cried Lean Leonard, who was visiting from a nearby town, "This is no cheese at all."

"I say it is," cried Robin, "and to prove it I'll drag it out."

"How will you do that?" Jack of Dover asked.

"I'll rake it up. My rake is nearby."

He brought his rake, walked to the middle of the bridge that was over the river, and began raking the water. But, no matter how much he tried, he only got dripping water, and everyone laughed.

"He who laughs last laughs best," cried Rich

48

Robin angrily. "I'll get that cheese and no one will cheat me of it."

Big John the blacksmith, who was Arthur's uncle, knew why the boy had sent Robin raking for the moon, and he wanted to help the lovers to be together a little longer. Besides, he was out to make a fool of Jack of Dover.

"Master Robin," said he, "your rake is not strong enough. You must fetch the cheese with your hands."

"How can I do that? The water is deep."

"I'll tell you a simple way," said John, and all listened.

"Look, I am strong, so I will hold you by your legs while you reach down and get the yellow cheese. You there, Harry, you must hold my legs, and that will make a chain of us long enough to get the rich prize."

Harry the vintner was a big fellow, even bigger than John, and ready to join in any game which promised a good laugh.

Said Harry, "I'll hold both of you."

49

John got hold of Robin's legs, and the cheeseman slid over the bridge. Next, big Harry got hold of John's legs, who also slid down. So Harry was holding John head down, and John was holding Master Robin head down, while his hands were deep in the water.

Suddenly John shouted, "Robin, my hands are slippery, I must wet them." He let go of Robin's legs and, plump, the cheeseman fell into the water!

Robin was fished out none the worse for the wetting, and his good wife Elizabeth made him go home for fear he would catch a cold. Both forgot their daughter, and that gave her a chance to be with Arthur and all the young people to play in the merry games of Midsummer Eve.

But for Jack of Dover there was little Midsummer Eve's joy. His reward from King John seemed only an image in the river, like the cheese that could never be got.

How the trivet
came home

TOL the draper needed a new trivet, one of those
three-legged stands with a round band, on the top of

8

which pots are put over the fire. So one day he went to Nottingham, which is famous for its smiths and ironworks. For there lived

> The little smith of Nottingham
> Who does the work that no men can.

With Tol was his white-and-black-spotted dog Trygg, running every way, as is the way of dogs. Tol spent his time in busy Nottingham talking and toasting, for, though not otherwise, he was a happy fellow.

In the humming market place he met a man from Sherwood Forest who was selling charcoal. He was a big, red-faced fellow named Allen, and Tol found him a jolly soul.

"Ah," said he, "I always wanted to be a big man, but here I am no bigger than Tom o' my Thumb."

"A little man but a good one," said Allen.

The two became friends at once, and when Tol had

52

bought his three-legged iron stand, both went to the inn. There they slowly ate a hearty meal, washing it down with good English ale and telling tales of Robin Hood. In the end Tol set out merrily, the trivet on his back, with his dog Trygg following. As for Allen, he stayed to meet another forester.

The day was amber hot, and soon the good fellow was bathed in perspiration from the weight of the iron and the walking.

Of a sudden he saw Jack of Dover coming along the road.

"Ho, there, Jack," he cried, "it's a day hot enough to broil the skin off your back. I say, a pox on this heat and this heavy iron."

"What of the heat?" replied Jack. "It's summer-time."

"Marry, you don't have to carry a heavy iron trivet on your back. A pox on this heat and the trivet, I say! A dog's life is better than mine. Look, there runs that big strong animal of mine, never doing a thing. I

53

wish he'd drag the trivet along the road instead of me carrying it on my tired back."

Trygg looked at his master, barked loudly, ran off a few paces, came back, and did the same over again.

"Ha, look ye, Jack, that's all he can do—bark, run, and eat, while I must carry iron on my sore back. I wish I were a dog with nothing to do save bark, run, and eat."

Said Jack, laughing, "There are those versed in black magic who can turn you quickly into a dog. I know where such a magician can be found."

"May the Lord preserve me from those who deal in the black art! I wouldn't come near 'em e'en for turning into a lion."

"Just think of the honor of being king of the beasts."

"Aye, 'tis a great honor, but I just don't like sleeping in the woods on dark nights."

Right then they passed a fine old green-leafed ash tree.

54

"King of the beasts or no king of the beasts, here I sit down and rest my weary bones till the sun sets," spoke Tol. "Then I'll go home. Come, Jack of Dover, sit down by my side and talk to me to while the time away."

Tol threw the trivet on the ground, and both sat down in the short grass against the tree, looking at the silver-blue sky with the white torn clouds floating in it. The dog ran to the nearby brook, took a lapping drink, and then swam about in the running water.

"I'd like to do the same as Trygg," said Tol. Then, after a time, " 'Twould seem that everyone has it better than I. There, look at that trivet! It has three strong iron legs and never moves, while I, with only two legs made of flesh and brittle bones, must carry it on my back this hot summer's day. The trivet should carry me home since I carried it half the way. That would be fair."

The trivet stood stock still while Trygg barked short barks.

55

"I never thought o' that," said Jack.

"We wise men of Gotham think of many things which men of other towns never think about," said Tol proudly.

"Aye, Tol, 'tis also said that you men of Gotham think and do the silliest deeds in all the land. Tell me truly, do you act silly just to fool King John of England? You can speak open with me, for I am your friend."

He said this hoping he'd find out the truth at last and then tell the tale to King John.

"Jack of Dover," said Tol testily, "'tis you who speak like a fool. We men of Gotham are honest men. As honest as any in the land, and I think it is most discourteous of you to speak so slightingly of us. Let's stop this silly clacking. I have more important affairs to attend to."

He turned to the trivet and addressed it:

"There you stand, you iron villain, without saying a word. The sun is low and I must hie home, for I am

56

getting hungry. Ah! I have an idea, Jack. That three-legged, stubborn dolt of a trivet thinks I'll carry it home. But I won't. I'll fool it. It'll have to do its own walking to my house."

Jack looked at Tol, eyes and mouth wide open, like a doleful owl.

"The trivet'll do its own walking home?" he said in surprise.

"Aye, it will. It has three legs, and I have only two, so it can walk better than I can." Then he turned to the trivet and said:

"Stand still if thou wilt, in the mayor's name, or follow me if thou wilt, and I can show you the right way home."

He arose and turned homeward, leaving the trivet standing on the ground. Jack of Dover looked and didn't know what to say. Now he was certain the people of Gotham were the silliest men in England.

"Ho, Tol, don't be such a fool," he cried. "Take the trivet along, or you'll lose it."

57

"I told you, Jack, that trivet can come along better than I can, and it will."

He kept on walking, and Jack followed without saying a word. So they came to Tol's house, where his wife stood at the gate.

"Husband, where is my trivet? Did you strike a good bargain?" she asked.

"I did indeed, wife. I am late coming for the heat and carrying of the heavy iron on my back."

"But where is my trivet?" she asked.

"It should be here," said Tol. "I told it to follow me."

"You told it to follow you?"

"I did, good wife. The sun shone hot, and I sat down under an ash tree to rest a little. Of a sudden I noticed the trivet had three strong iron legs, while I had only two of soft flesh. So I asked it to follow me instead of my dragging it on my sore back."

"Mistress," cried Jack of Dover, "did you ever hear of anything more silly?"

58

"It has three legs, and I have only two, so it can walk better than I."

"It's not silly at all, Master Jack of Dover. If my husband Tol says that the trivet is on its way home, then it is on its way home. My husband never tells a lie." Then she turned to her husband. "Where left you the trivet?"

"At Gotham Hill."

"Methinks I'll run and help it come home."

"Nay, you needn't, good wife, it'll find its way, I am certain. It can follow my footsteps. Besides, I'm hungry. Let's stand here at the gate and wait for it and welcome it."

"Nay, I think I'll run and see how far it's come, husband."

She turned her steps to the road and had gone but a short way when she saw two men coming toward her. . . .

Now, along the road which Tol had taken came Allen, the charcoal seller, and another forester. They passed the ash tree where Tol and Jack had sat.

61

"By Robin Hood's bow! If it isn't the trivet my jolly little friend Tol bought this morning," said Allen.

"Finding is keeping," growled the other.

"Don't say that. The fellow who lost or left the trivet is kind and friendly. This morning he and I ate bread together. I don't know for what reason he left it here, but I'll take it to Gotham and give it to him."

He picked it up, and they went toward Gotham way, and soon they saw coming toward them Tol's wife. She saw the trivet.

"Found you this iron trivet at Gotham Hill?" she asked.

"That we did, good woman," Allen said.

"Then it's the one my husband left. I'll thank ye if ye give it to me."

Allen did, and she thanked him and hurried homeward. When Tol saw his wife coming, pulling the trivet behind her, he cried: "Ha, Master Jack, didn't I tell you the trivet'd come walking home?"

62

"Fool's luck," grumbled Jack.

"I wouldn't call it fool's luck," said Tol. "It's Gotham luck." And Jack of Dover was so bewildered that all he could say was:

> Laws-a-dees,
> What times be these.

Hasty porridge in the boiling water

THE days galloped on, the months rolled by, and still Jack of Dover had not learned if the men of

Gotham were wise or otherwise. Yet was he most anxious to make his report to King John and earn his money for spying. More and more he stayed near Gotham to watch for that which he wanted to happen.

On a day, a kind of day the bees love dearly, some Gotham men and Jack of Dover were walking along the rushing river that was whirling around and smashing at stones and the green bank.

They came to a turn of the road where the contrary current of the racing river caused the water to boil and spout and hiss as if it were a whirlpool or a bubbling cauldron.

"See how the water boils," cried Giles the goose-man.

"If we had plenty of oatmeal," said John the black-smith, laughing loudly, "we might make hasty porridge to serve the village for a month."

"There's a good idea," cried Robin the cheese-man. "Why not do it?"

65

"Pindy-pandy, man!" said Jack of Dover, not trusting his own ears. "You'd not do that."

"That I would, indeed," said Robin testily. "We men of Gotham are no sillies and we do things better than any men in England. Go, Jack of Dover, go to the fair and get you a cock-a-hoop till you learn better."

John the blacksmith watched Jack of Dover from the corner of his eye.

Then Robin and fat Ned, Tol the draper, and Tom the tinker resolved to go to the village and fetch the oatmeal. John and Jack and another remained at the river.

Soon the four men of Gotham returned with the oatmeal in pots and bags.

Jack of Dover watched and thought: Now I'll see if they throw the oatmeal in the running river. Surely they won't throw the good food away to act silly. But John the blacksmith was clever as he was big and read easily what was in Jack's mind.

Said Tol, "Into the water with the oatmeal, and

66

none will have to cook hasty porridge for many a week."

So the oatmeal was thrown into the boiling water while the men stood by watching.

The water hissed and foamed white while the grain turned every which way till it was sucked up by the water altogether.

"How shall we know when the porridge is ready?" cried Tom the tinker.

"Why, that's simple as sleeping. Let one of us jump in and taste it, and if it is found ready for eating let him signify it to us standing on the shore. You, Tom, jump in." So spoke Giles.

Tom leaped in, but the water was much deeper than he thought. Two times he rose, but never said one word. Those standing on the bank became impatient. Seeing Tom smacking his lips, which he did to catch his breath, they thought it signified he was enjoying the food and asking them to come too. They leaped in, one after the other.

Now, John knew well the man was drowning and

67

would not let it be so. Whereupon he leaped in the circling water and cried to the others:

"Swim with me below the bend where we can't be seen by Jack. Forget the oatmeal." Then he took hold of Tom and swam with him to the safe place, while the others, carried by the swift current of the water, were pulled also behind the bend, well washed and well wetted for their silliness.

But Jack of Dover, who stayed on the shore, said the men had drowned. He told it to one, who told it to all, and so it was told thenafter and set down in the books.

68

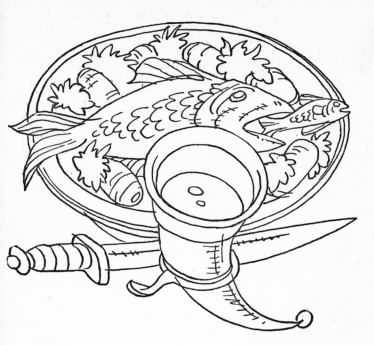

The little fish and the big fish

IN THE fall of the year, when Jack of Dover was on the road, he met Harry the vintner of Gotham.

10

"Where are you going, vintner?" shouted Jack of Dover.

"To Oxford town, to visit my brother, who is a blacksmith by trade."

"Let the two of us travel together, for two are better company than one along a dusty road."

The two men walked side by side, shortening the distance by leagues with their merry talk and their gay laughter.

When they came to Oxford, each went his own way—Harry the vintner going to his brother's house, and Jack of Dover to his friend's.

Now, Jack of Dover traveled among rich people even as among the poor. He was welcomed by all for his merry tales and shrewd wit, and for that reason he was invited to dine, the next great festival day, at the table of a nobleman who lived some two miles from the town.

On the set day, while riding to the nobleman's house, he once again met Harry the vintner and his brother James the blacksmith, who was a big fellow, a merry and conceited one, and full of jests, just the same as his brother, Harry of Gotham.

"Ha, there, Jack of Dover! Greetings! Where to?" said Harry and James.

"Friends, I'm on my way to eat a fine meal," replied the restless rover. "It's at the home of the most generous lord of the town. Come along, unbidden but welcome ne'ertheless. Where there's room for many, there's always room for two more." He thought the vintner would do some silly act at dinner that would give all a good laugh.

Thus they came to the chamber, where a great company was gathered. There were present knights and squires, merchantmen and famous artisans.

When the host heard that they had for a guest one of the men of Gotham, renowned for their silly deeds, and his brother James, well known for his nimble wit, he thought to have some jests with them. For he was a merry man himself and a lover of a good laugh.

71

He sat James the blacksmith and Harry the vintner together not far from him amongst the noble company.

Many rich foods were brought to the table, among them a large platter with two gurnet fish. One was very large, and one, lying in the mouth of the large fish, was very small, put there for an ornament.

The lord took the little fish, placed it on a big plate, and set it before the two brothers. Now, both the brothers loved good food and were very hungry. They looked with a long face at the little fish, small as a small finger, and all the company also looked to see what the two would do. They were ready for a good laugh.

The brothers looked at each other and put their heads together, speaking for a time. Next, James picked up the little fish with two fingers, but, instead of putting it into his mouth, he put it near his ear. Then, after a time, he gave it to Harry, who did the very same thing.

72

"The little fish says he cannot tell us these things because he is too young," said the blacksmith.

The host and the company wondered at the strange behavior.

Asked the lord, "Ha, good fellows, do ye put food in your ears instead of in your mouths?"

"My lord," said the blacksmith, "I am not eating at all, nor is my brother; we are listening instead."

"Listening! Listening to what?" asked the lord.

"To the fish, my lord. To that little fish, from whom we would learn the news of a friend of ours who drowned not long ago."

"Is the little spiced fish telling it to you?" the nobleman asked.

"No, he is not, my lord. The little fish says he cannot tell us these things because he is too young, but that the big fellow on your platter knows all about it. Therefore, I beseech your lordship to send the big fish here instead."

Whether the fellow said this from shrewdness, or whether he truly meant it, is known only to the wise of the world. But what everyone did know was that

75

the brothers were quickly served with the big piece of fish before all the others.

On the way home Harry the vintner met Jack of Dover again. Jack was more eager than ever to learn if the men of Gotham truly were silly or whether they were just acting that way.

"Tell me, Harry, and tell me truly," he said, "did you and your brother hear that little fish talking, or did you just say that to the nobleman to get a good big piece of fish?"

"Jack," spoke Harry, "you are forever trying to learn the business of the people of Gotham, and we are not certain why. You're a smart fellow and have traveled many miles, which I have not. Certes you are shrewder than I am. And since you who are shrewd cannot tell if the men of Gotham act silly to gain an end or because they are sillies, how can I tell, who am just a silly man from Gotham town?"

So Jack went his way still uncertain of whether the wise men of Gotham were fooling him or were fools.

But I bet you know.

Grazing on the roof

ONE day Jack of Dover and a nobleman came to Gotham. They rode proud horses, their rich clothes flamed in the sun, and they went straight to Richard the alderman.

"We were sent by the King to see if the people of Gotham were happy," they said.

But they really came to hide some money for King John which he had taken from the people.

King John couldn't think of a better place to conceal his gold than in the town of silly folk. It surely would be safe there.

After a few days, Jack and the nobleman decided the best place to hide the money would be right in the alderman's house, where no one would think of looking for it.

They chose as the proper spot the chimney on the roof, which was all covered with thick moss, as were most of the roofs of Gotham.

One dark night, when the alderman and many of the townspeople were at a meeting in the town hall, Jack climbed up to the roof, loosened a few of the bricks of the chimney under the moss, and put the

78

bag with the money there. The nobleman, high on his horse, was on the lookout.

Now, young Arthur, who loved Grace, the cheeseman's daughter, chose the same time to see his sweetheart. They were talking at the gate when Elizabeth, Grace's mother, called her, and the lovers had to part.

Arthur ran off and passed by Alderman Richard's house. He saw the man on the roof, heard him talking to the man on the horse, and learned their secret.

When the two were gone, Arthur hurried to the meeting.

At first he was for telling to all what he had seen and heard. But then he remembered that it was not good for a common man to tell a noble's secrets. He thought it better to speak only to the alderman.

The next day he told the tale to Richard. The alderman praised him for his silence at the meeting,

79

for he said to have spoken then might have done harm to the whole town. Then he cautioned Arthur not to breathe a word to anyone until he had thought more about it.

Soon Jack of Dover and the noble left, and Richard the alderman decided that since King John had stolen the hidden money from the people, the men of Gotham had a greater right to it than the King.

But it was dangerous to take something that belonged to the King. Even if it were never known who took it, the alderman would be accountable for it, since it was in his house. More likely, all the town would be punished for it. Such were the harsh laws of those days.

But if the money were found by accident and divided openly among the people, they might not be punished at all. Yet no thought of how to do it would come to him.

One day some of the townsfolk of Gotham and

80

the alderman were standing before his house talking of this and that. Amongst them was Robert the herald, who happened to be there.

Tol the draper, one of the Gothamites, had been looking for a time at the roof of the house, all covered with moss and green.

All of a sudden Tol said, "Look at your roof, Master Alderman, it is all covered with grass, good enough for a cow to graze."

"So it is," said Richard.

"Why not graze your cow there and have her grow fat on't?"

"How will ye get the cow on the roof?" queried the herald.

"Why, thou silly fellow," replied Tol, " 'tis a very simple thing. I'd hoist the cow up, as 'tis done with a big stone."

"You would never do that!" said the herald.

"And why not?" asked Tol. "It's a pity to let the good green food go to waste."

81

"But what of the cow! She'll surely choke in the pulling."

"Nay, she'll not, she'll be too busy chewing and have little time to think of choking."

"I tell ye it will kill that cow," said the herald.

"No, 'twon't."

"There'll be no arguing when the cow's dead."

"Never fear, good herald. What do you think on this, Master Alderman?"

Richard had listened to the argument and never said a word, but there was a smile on his face. Now he spoke up.

"I think like Tol the draper," he said quickly.

Again the herald argued against choking the cow, but the more he tried to stop the others, the more set they seemed on it.

In the end, Robert decided that the men of Gotham were the worst fools in the world and that he could not teach them any wisdom.

Richard led his cow out of the stable, put a rope

All of a sudden, down came the cow and the chimney—and a shower of gold and silver coins with it.

around her neck, and threw the end of it over the chimney.

By then many people had gathered about.

The cow stood quietly at one side, while the folk of Gotham stood at the other. As for Robert the herald, he was in great anger, but he could do nothing.

The men got hold of the loose end of the rope and began pulling.

Up went the cow, kicking her legs in the air and growling and gurgling from the tightening of the rope.

Women began to scream, and children began to cry, when, all of a sudden, down came the cow and the chimney that was not strong enough to hold the animal—and a shower of gold and silver coins with it!

There was a wild rush for the money, but Alderman Richard cried:

"Halt! Half of it goes to me and half to the people."

The money was divided, and the alderman gave Arthur part of his own share.

85

Soon after, Jack of Dover came looking for the money. When he heard the tale of the cow grazing on the roof and heard what had happened to the shower of gold that had come from the chimney, his anger knew no bounds. He cried vengeance and cursed the Gotham folk for fools. But the people just laughed at him and said 'twas not his gold anyway.

As for the King, he never sent for the money, for he would not have it known he hid money in such places.

John the blacksmith destroys the wasps in the straw

ALONG the yellow, dusty road came Jack of Dover on a big gray horse, and beside him rode the good chaplain of Nottingham on a glossy brown mule. They were talking of this and that, but mostly of the men of Gotham, whether they were silly noodles or feigning silliness to do as they pleased and thus gain their ends. So they arrived in Gotham and, just as chance would have it, when they neared John the blacksmith's shop, they saw one of the Gotham townsmen coming the same way, leading his horse and talking to the animal:

"Now, I must have you shod once again. A pox on you! Here I shod you just two weeks past in Nottingham, and in the wink of an eye a shoe falls off. Blacksmiths are no longer what they used to be. Your carcass isn't worth what you cost me."

Saying this, he entered the big doors of the smithy.

"I smell some silly act," said Jack of Dover. "Why don't we go into the smithy and see, Chaplain? We can go on a little later."

"Gladly, Jack," the Chaplain said; "I find you good company and I am ever ready for a good jest."

88

The two alighted from their animals, tied them to a post, and went into the smithy.

Now, John the blacksmith of Gotham was a big, broad man, afraid of nothing and ready to help all. His face was red and his beard was black, and when he laughed, the rafters shook like tall trees in the wind, for his smithy was very old—almost ready to fall down.

When he shod the horse of a poor man he asked no pay, and for this he was liked and trusted by all.

John greeted the two with a smile and then spoke to his townsman:

"I'll be done quickly with your good horse, and I promise you the shoe'll wear out 'stead of fall off."

He set to work eagerly, for John loved to hear his hammer ring and see the sparks a-flying. Clank! Clang! rang the heavy iron on the anvil. It was a merry song, and the sparks danced around in tune.

In the straw, at one end of the ceiling of John's forge, was a wasps' nest. The day was warm, and the

89

wasps flew busily in and out of their home. In the end, one of them sat on Jack's nose and stung him fiercely.

Jack screamed with pain and roared, "My nose! How dare you have wasps here? My nose! It stings! Get those wasps out. You are not worthy to keep a forge."

"Master Jack," replied John, "I can't order the wasps about, they won't obey."

"That's true," said the chaplain, trying to hide a smile.

Soon a few more wasps were buzzing around Jack's thin nose.

"Villain, I say get those wasps out. I order you. Do it at once. Destroy their nest! If you lose anything thereby, I'll pay for it." He meant the wasps' nest. "Lord! Here they are again!"

"Master Jack," said John, "if you say that, I'll drive the wasps so far they'll never come back. But you all must leave while I do it." Jack and the chaplain and the townsmen went out followed by the horse.

Then John took the black iron coulter and heated it to a glowing red in his forge. When it was the color of white fire, he thrust it into the nest that was in the straw, shouting, "This for the wasps!" Then he went out where the three men stood. At once the nest and the straw around it began to burn. Before you could say the Lord's prayer, the smithy was on fire, and soon the wooden shed was burned down.

"Do you see, Jack of Dover," John cried lustily while the house was burning, "those wasps will never trouble you again. Now, you promised to pay if I lost anything thereby, and so you must build me a new smithy."

"What, you villain?" cried Jack. "Have you lost your wits?"

"I have not," said John in a mocking tone. "Weren't these your words? You said if I lost anything thereby, you'd pay for it. I have witnesses."

91

"I meant damage to the wasps' nest," cried Jack.

"You did not say that," said John. "You said if I lost anything by destroying their nest you'd pay for it. I have witnesses, my neighbor and this good chaplain."

"Those were your words, Jack," the chaplain said smilingly. "One must be careful of promises made even to . . . fools."

Jack made a dour face. He liked to laugh at the foolish deeds of the men of Gotham but not to pay for them. Yet he had given his word, and he could not deny it, so he promised John he'd build him a new smithy.

When he was on the road with the chaplain, he said:

"Do you think that fellow was really a fool, or did he burn his forge on purpose?"

"Friend," answered the chaplain with a smile, "in Gotham foolish and wise things seem the same."

Rolling cheese gathers
no moss

THIS is how it happened:
  Robin the cheeseman of Gotham was walking on a

13

day filled with sun and song to Nottingham market.
On his shoulders was a load of round, buttery cheeses,
and on his forehead big beads of slithery perspiration,
for the weight was heavy. So he came to the top of a
hill and began walking down, when one of the cheeses
fell out of the bag and went rolling down the hill.

Robin was a man quick to lose his temper. "By
bulls and bait," he shouted, "had I known this! Here
I've been carrying you heavy cheeses while the sun
is broiling my flesh, and now you show me how you
can run to the market alone! Why didn't you tell me
this before? It would have saved me all the work this
hot summer's day. But it's none too late. The rest of
you cheeses can go alone to market."

He slid the sack off his back and, taking out the
other four cheeses, sent them tumbling one after the
other. Some rolled into one bush, some into another,
and all found a resting place on the bright green
grass.

Said Robin, "I charge all of you to meet me in the
market place where I always stand, in front of the

butter stall near the church." Then he set off light-heartedly, for the load was off his back and walking was much easier.

Robin came to the Nottingham "woman's market," where he always stood. It was near the church, by Ursula's butter stall. There she was in a green kirtle, squatting before a basket of eggs and pads of butter covered with broad vine leaves.

"A good day to you, dame," he cried. "Have my cheeses come to the market?"

"Cheeses?" said she. "What cheeses?"

"My cheeses, those that went to the market; they know the way well enough."

"Robin," said Mistress Ursula, "you've gone off your head. Or perhaps you've been too long at the inn."

This made Robin angry. He shouted at her, and in the end he blamed all the world because his cheeses were not there.

Then he searched for them everywhere and asked all the merchants and the people who came to buy—

95

amongst whom was Jack of Dover—if they had not seen his cheeses come to market.

"Who brought them?" all asked.

"Marry, they brought themselves," said Robin. "The first one rolled down the hill toward Nottingham, and I sent the others after him. Lord! They went fast enough. Ha, perhaps they ran so fast they couldn't stop themselves. A vengeance on them! Maybe they ran beyond the market place. I am now fully persuaded that they be now almost at York."

"That might be," said Jack of Dover with a wink in his eye. "Perhaps they are now for certain at the York market."

"That's it," said Robin. "They rolled very fast, and they must be in York by now; I'll go and see."

So he hired a horse and rode to York to find the cheeses, while Jack of Dover, leading the men of Nottingham, ran the other way to look for them, too. For, as one could say, never let a rolling cheese gather moss.

96

But when they got there, there were no cheeses any-where, and this is the reason why.

Soon after Robin had rolled his cheeses down the hill, Arthur, his son-in-law, came by the place on horseback with a bag of gloves to be delivered in York.

He saw the cheeses, and by their marks he knew them to be his father-in-law's. Never asking how they came there, for he was used to the strange ways of his father-in-law, he picked them up, loaded them on his horse, and went to York, where he sold them at a good price. When Arthur was done with all his business, Robin arrived in York, asking all whether they had seen his cheeses. When he saw Arthur, he asked him the same question.

"Indeed I have," said Arthur, "and sold them at a good price."

Robin was much pleased at this and, without asking any questions, the two set off to Gotham.

When they came to Nottingham, in order that

Robin might return the horse, Jack and the towns-people were back from looking for the cheeses.

"Why were you seeking my cheeses?" asked Robin. "Didn't I tell you, Jack, they rolled to the York market? That is just what they did, and my son-in-law Arthur sold them at a good price."

The men of Nottingham looked and looked and couldn't understand. Jack was so angry he could have jumped out of his skin.

"Fool's luck," he cried.

"That's better than sly fellow's disappointment," said Arthur, looking at Jack.

And to this day the hill near Nottingham down which Robin rolled his cheeses is known as "Cheese Hill." You can see it when you go there.

Never trust an
eel

ALL England knew by then of the silly men of
Gotham, but Jack of Dover still said they were only

14

shamming silliness in order to gain their own ends.

He never stopped coming to their town for one reason or another to learn if they were playing a double game.

One time during Lent, when some people do not eat meat, he brought a few baskets of white herrings, red herrings, sprats, and other salted fish to sell to the people of Gotham.

Now, the people of Gotham loved salted fish, and they bought so many of them that when Lent was over they still had plenty left. But now they wanted to eat good beef pies and mutton, and they didn't know what to do with the left-over fish.

They cast their heads together, considering what to do with their white herrings, their red herrings, their sprats and other salted fish.

"Why not eat it all in one day?" said John the blacksmith.

Lean Leonard, whose long neck on his head waved like a wheat stalk, agreed. He could eat for three.

100

Jack of Dover was still there, too, hearing all this, and so the wise men of Gotham were wary.

Spoke big John the blacksmith, "Friends, don't let us eat these good, salted fish, but let's use them to make money and give us fish next Lent."

"How can we do that?" asked Robin the cheese-man.

"Ha, I know. Let us put the dead fish in our pond and let them breed," cried Giles. "They will bear enough salted fish for us to eat and to sell."

"That's a fine idea, Giles," said Robin.

Richard the alderman growled but said nothing.

Spoke Arthur, laughing: "I say the same as Giles. Let us cast these fish into the pond which is in the middle of our town, that they may increase against the next year."

Then each man went home and brought the fish he had left, to cast them into the pond.

Said one Gothamite: "I have thus many white her-rings."

Said another: "I have thus many red herrings."

Said others: "I have thus many sprats."

Said others: "I have thus many salt fishes."

Then they all cried: "Let them all go into the pond. We shall fare like lords the next Lent."

Thereupon they all threw their salted and dried dead fish into the green water.

Jack went to Nottingham and told everyone what fools the men of Gotham were, and many promised to come and see this sort of fishing for dead herring.

The year went 'round, and the holy Lent season was near, so Jack of Dover with a good number of men of Nottingham came to Gotham to see the sport.

The men of Gotham were ready with a big net.

Robin and the others threw the net into the pond and let it lie there for a time. Then Robin cried, "Pull," and the net rose slowly.

And what do you think was in it? No white herrings, no red herrings, no sprats, no salted fish of any kind, only—a very fat, very long eel! The biggest and fattest eel anyone had ever seen. All winter he had eaten the dead salted fish and had grown as big and fat as a sea serpent. The women and children were so scared they ran halfway down the meadow. Even some of the men were a little afraid of the big fish.

But Robin shouted, "Look at the giant beast! He ate up all our good herrings. I'll burn him, the robber! I'll hang him! I'll quarter him!"

"No," said his wife Elizabeth, who was as wise as her husband, "let us drown the beast that stole our good profit."

"Drown he should for his crime," cried another.

"Slow drowning, say I," cried a third, while Jack of Dover and the citizens of Nottingham there present looked on with open mouths and goggling eyes.

The alderman was silent for a time, then he roared, "Be it so," and all roared the same.

Thereupon they went to the other pond, a larger one, dragging the eel on the grassy ground, and threw him into the water.

103

No sooner did the eel feel the cool wet than he began wriggling right and left, left and right.

"Ah! look how he suffers," cried one.

Other shouted, "Serves him right. Lie there and shift for yourself. No help will you get from us. Drown in misery!" And they left the eel to drown.

Said a man from Nottingham, "Jack of Dover, here your long search for the biggest fool in merry England is ended, for none could be more silly than these men of Gotham."

"Methinks," said Jack of Dover, "they work too hard at being silly, which makes me doubt their silliness."

He went away shaking his head and mumbling, while the folk of Nottingham went away shaking with laughter. You and I know who were the wisest there.

The hare and the lord

EACH year the people of Gotham paid rent to their
lord who lived in Newark, and this year it was given

15

to Robin the cheeseman to take it there in person.

Now, Robin was so busy thinking of new ways to do old things that he forgot all about going with the money until the day before the payment was due, which was too short a time to bring it to Newark.

The lord was a strict man when it came to rents, and Robin knew he and the whole town would suffer if the money were late.

The cheeseman ran out on the green, crying to young and old about his forgetfulness and the dire trouble that would come of it.

Many Gothamites gathered around him and were ready to weep with misery.

Cried one, "Tomorrow is our pay day, and what remedy shall we find to send our money to our lord?"

Cried another, "It will go hard with us, this forgetfulness. We must find a way."

So the talk went back and forth, and in the end Robin the cheeseman said:

"Friends, but a week ago Arthur, my son-in-law,

106

brought me a fine fat hare. He shall carry it for us. He is very light of foot. This very day he shall carry the money to our lord."

"Be it so," said the others.

"Fine," chimed Robin the cheeseman. "I'll go fetch the hare and bring the purse with the money. Meanwhile you men write the letter which we will send with the purse."

Robin ran home while the good citizens of Gotham set to work on the letter. Though it was short in words, it was long in writing, but in the end it was done.

They tied the purse with the money and the letter around the hare's neck, and then Robin spoke to the hare:

"Listen and hear, little beast! I am trusting you with a message of great importance, and if you do it well, I will spare your life and that of your children. Now, run as fast as your legs will carry you; first to Loughborough, then to Leicester, and then to New-

107

ark, where you'll find our lord in his rich castle. Commend us to him and deliver to him the letter and the money. When you've done this, you may roam once again over hill and dale, and I swear to you no one will ever trouble you."

He let the hare loose, and it flew off like an arrow —in the opposite direction.

"Ho, there, nimblefoot," Mistress Robin shouted. "Ho, there, we told you to go to Loughborough first."

"Nay," cried Robin, "let the hare alone. He is going off the regular roads to keep away from hunters and dogs. He can tell the nearest way better than any of us. Let him go."

Then Robin and his wife went to sleep in peace and joy.

Two weeks later the lord came to the alderman in great anger, demanding his money.

Richard went at once with the nobleman to Robin and asked him what he had done with the money. Thereupon Robin related how he and the other Goth-

"Now the hare has a bag of money and your letter to our lord," said Arthur.

amites after due deliberation had sent the money and letter.

When the lord heard how the the rent had been sent with the hare, he laughed till the tears ran down his eyes. Yet he demanded the money, adding:

"The hare must have taken the money to market to buy cabbages and carrots. When we catch him, we'll punish him for his thievery."

"You, Robin, must pay all the money," the alderman said angrily.

Robin was ready to weep, for he loved his gold dearly, but he went to his strong chest. As he was about to open it, in rushed Arthur, his son-in-law, shouting:

"Here is a strange thing. I snared once again the very same hare I gave to you, Father Robin, but now it has a bag of money and your letter to our lord."

Robin fell around Arthur's neck in sheer joy.

"The Lord watches over us," said Mistress Robin.

"Truly, the Heavenly Lord watches over the men

III

of Gotham," said the nobleman. "I've heard it said Jack of Dover is forever spying on you for King John, who bears you a grudge."

"That's true indeed, but it will do him little good, Messire," spoke Arthur, "for the men of Gotham have a nimble wit; they pray to the Lord in Heaven and live in peace with the world. If all the cities in the land would do the same, they'd be as merry as we."

The lord went off, contented with his money and with a smile on his face. He did not love King John, either, and he was pleased to find citizens who could outwit the King as well as his henchmen.

Tall tales from
Gotham Inn

WINTER had come to Gotham, and the wind sang songs around doors while the snow danced. Inside the houses big fires were burning, giving forth warmth and the smell of good food.

One day, soon after Christmas, the citizens of Gotham were gathered in the inn to tell tales and laugh at good jests. Of a sudden the door opened and a wild gust of wind drove in a cloud of snow, a sackful of cold, and wily Jack of Dover.

He shook the snow from his broad shoulders, smiled, and shouted, "Ha, there, merry men of Gotham, greetings to you, wide as a sailing ship on the sea."

And since it was the merry yuletide, they were glad to see him, though they did not trust him. But aside from that they knew he was a man ever ready for a rollicking tale and a bright quip. They welcomed him heartily, bade him sit down and partake of food and drink.

"Good fellow, from where do you come this wild and wintry day?" asked Richard the alderman.

"I come from Herford and from Oxford and from

many towns besides. Thus I roam seeking the fool of fools and gathering joyous tales and wise saws to be told wherever there is good company and good food."

"And what tales have you gathered of late, Jack of Dover?" cried the good men of Gotham.

"Tales that'll tickle your ribs and open your eyes and pale your lips and cause you cries of laughter."

"Out with them, man. It's a day for just such pastimes. A good and merry tale we want that'll give us a girthful of mirth." That from all sides.

"You shall have one according to your demand. A roaring tale and broad as our land from coast to coast. Those who don't believe it may eat salt from the sea, rocks from the mountains, and thorns from the bushes. So here goes: A little time ago I was in Herford. Do you know the town?"

"I was there three years ago," cried Cutting Tom.

"Then you surely know the church steeple of Burndwood in Essex. One night, three weeks ago, that church steeple sailed all by itself across the sea to Calais, which is a city in France, and then back again to Burndwood to its proper place. Remember, friends, all in the space of a single night. I saw the steeple with my own eyes. A gentleman in Herford believed this to be truth, and I am sure you do, as well."

There were oh's and ah's. Then Tol the draper piped:

"We believe your tale and know you tell the truth, Jack of Dover, though we never saw such marvel with our own eyes. But, then, you're a man who's traveled far and wide."

"That I have," said Jack of Dover, "up and down our merry England."

Said John the blacksmith, "I haven't traveled up and down our merry England, I've been in Gotham all my life, and I can tell you as good a story and as true a one."

Everyone laughed, and there were cries all around:

116

"Another time, John; this time we would hear what Jack of Dover has to tell."

So Jack began again:

"Here's a tale heard around Sherwood Forest in Nottinghamshire. One day, and not so long ago, five hundred of the King of Spain's ships sailed into the Sherwood Forest in Nottinghamshire to besiege Robin Hood's dell. But after them came forty thousand scholars with eldern switches and broke the gallant ships to pieces and overthrew them as if they were so many stalks of straw. There was a valiant piece of work for you, and the Herford gentlemen believed that, too—surely you will as well."

" 'Twas indeed so," cried Giles. "I know the tale, and I've told it, too. Do you know of any others?"

"I do indeed. I made the selfsame gentleman in Herford believe that Westminster Hall in London fell under great suspicion of treason against the English realm and that the stone building was banished for ten years into Staffordshire."

117

"Served the traitor right," cried Robin, red as fire.

"Now, listen to what happened just two days ago to a tinker in Canterbury; it's the best of all," said Jack.

"What was that?" all cried.

"You know William the glover there, don't you?"

"I know him for a fine man," said Arthur.

"Well, there were twenty-two children born to him in one year."

Said Tol:

"I believed every word you told, Jack, but not this last tale."

"You can go there and see 'em all for yourself," said Jack.

The wind blew fierce, and the sky was dark, so Tol would not go right then to Canterbury to find out if Jack of Dover had told the truth or had not told the truth.

Next day the morning was bright and sunny, and Jack of Dover left, seeking the fool of fools in England.

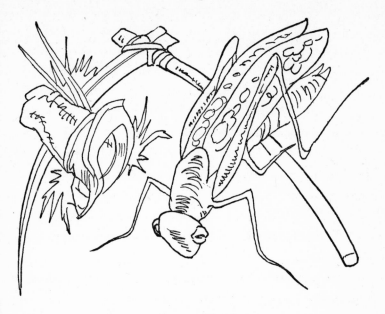

The devil in
the wheat

GOLDEN sunshine and warm summer wind covered the fields around Gotham. Tol, the little

doughty draper, had left his home and was a-mowing in the meads. Swish! sang the gleaming scythe through the warm air; swash! it flashed through the thick, heavy, nodding stalks. So Tol went along, laying down swath after swath of golden grain while the sweat ran down his face.

Suddenly he saw leaping through the ripe wheat a great green monster! A giant grasshopper, big as a goat, hopping toward him! It took three great hops, then it stopped, sitting down, its long green legs high in the air, its thick, green, ogling eyes staring straight at the draper.

Black fright seized the good man. He dropped his scythe as if 'twere on fire, and he took to the road, shouting:

"There's a fiend in the field dressed like a grasshopper. He wants to devour me. To arms! Help! Friends! Neighbors!"

Up the road came Jack of Dover, a pack on his horse and dust all over.

120

"What ails you, friend Tol?" he cried.

"There's a devil in my field in the guise of a great green grasshopper! He wants to destroy me! I'm on my way to Gotham to fetch my neighbors for help." He kept on running along the road, crying all the time:

"Come, neighbors! Come, friends! Help me drive the devil away! Help! Alarum!"

Jack of Dover followed slowly on the horse, not knowing what to make of it. Soon Tol was in the town, and his cries brought men and women, friends and neighbors with clubs, staves, halberds, and sundry other kinds of murderous weapons. They were all ready to help kill the fierce fiend in the guise of a green grasshopper that was in Tol's wheat field.

So they set out, a long line of armed Gotham men dressed in fustian and red, hosen and jerkins, Tol leading the way. Jack of Dover ambled along on his horse. But the nearer the good men got to the mead where the giant grasshopper was hid in the rippling wheat, the slower and slower and slower they ran. Tol came to the field and, hearing no sound behind him, turned around and saw his neighbors lagging behind. He ran back and cried:

"Why tarry ye? Come, help me destroy the devil in my mead."

Jack of Dover rode up to the field, but, look as he would, he could see no grasshopper devil there. He turned back and shouted:

"Where is that devil?"

"Right in the field, hiding in the thick stalks," cried Tol.

But the men of Gotham were standing still. Said one to the other:

"Let every man cross himself against this grasshopper devil. We will not meddle with him."

"What?" cried Jack of Dover. "You'll let little Tol battle singlehanded the green devil in the mead?"

"Only fools meddle with devils; wise men keep at home," one cried, and turned back to the village. The others followed quickly. The whole procession was going the other way.

"Come!" cried Tol, "ye won't e'en help me get my good scythe?"

"No," the men of Gotham said. "It is good to sleep in a whole skin. Better you lose your scythe than we our lives."

Now, Jack of Dover surely could not tell whether such behavior was silly or wise, for he was only looking for gain, that ever blinds reason.

Gotham way of counting

ON a crystal-blue day in May, twelve men of Gotham, such as favored talking more than working,

18

went a-fishing early in the morning. They came to a hurrying brook, and some went wading in the waters while others stood upon the dry land and caught a fine mess of glistening fish.

This put them in a merry mood and set their wet tongues a-wagging about the fine fish supper they soon would have.

So, tongues clacking, they went homeward with joy in their hearts and no care in their minds. Of a sudden Giles the gooseman stopped.

"Marry," quoth he, "we all ventured fearlessly this morning wading in the water. I pray to God that none of us who came from home be drowned."

"By Robin Hood! Let us count one the others and see, for there were twelve of us came out this morning. I'll count ye." This, from Robin the cheeseman.

They all stood up in a row, Robin right before them, and he slowly began to count them. But he forgot to count himself and so found they were only eleven men instead of twelve.

125

"Alas!" cried he to the others. "There is one of us drowned."

"Mayhap you did not count right," said Fat Ned. "I'll count this time."

Fat Ned numbered the men, not adding himself, just as Robin had done, and he, too, counted only eleven.

Now all were certain that one had drowned, and they wept salty tears.

They went back to the brook where they had been wading and fishing and sought up and down and all around for him that was drowned, and when they could not find him they did make a great lamentation.

While they stood around, down the road came Jack of Dover, Richard the alderman, and a courtier of the King. Richard and Jack had been talking of the men of Gotham, and they were in one another's hair.

Jack said he was in search of the fool of fools, mak-

126

ing his inquiries in most of the principal places in England.

But Richard said Jack was spying on the honest men of Gotham. Added he:

"When you've done seeking fools amongst people, you'll be adjudged the biggest fool of all for doing that."

"Well," cried Jack, "come what may, I'm still wise enough not to be fooled by the men of your town playing the fool to fool the King."

'Twas near dark when they came upon the motley men of Gotham a-weeping and a-wailing for the one that was drowned. No sooner did they see the alderman than Robin cried:

"Woe unto us, one of us drowned."

"Lord-a-mercy! How did that happen?" asked Richard.

"Alas, Richard! This day we went a-fishing in the brook, and there did come twelve of us, but now there are only eleven of us. One of us has drowned."

127

"What makes ye say one has drowned?" said Jack of Dover in surprise, for he had seen there were twelve present.

"We counted one the other seven times over, and each time we found there were only eleven present."

"Ye counted well?" said Richard.

"That we did," said Fat Ned. "I did the counting, and if you don't believe it, I'll do it over again right now, and you'll see that one of us is drowned."

He began telling them off, exactly as he did before, counting eleven men but not himself.

"There," he cried, "there are only eleven of us."

The courtier and Jack looked at each other, then at Richard, and in the end at the men of Gotham.

"Well," quoth Jack of Dover, "this to my mind is pretty foolery."

"Go back to King John and tell him this," said Richard.

"Maybe they are just playing the fool," said Jack of Dover.

"We'll find out!" said the nobleman.

Then he turned to the men of Gotham, "What will ye give me if I find the twelfth man?"

"Sir," said they, "we'll give you all the money we have."

"Then give me your money," the noble said, "for I promise ye here, in the name of the Lord, I'll find ye the man who drowned."

Thereupon each man emptied his wallet, which was not very much, while Jack and Richard just looked on.

"Now," said the nobleman, "stand in a line as ye did before." This they did, whereat the courtier came up to them and gave the first one a hard blow on his shoulder, which made the fellow groan. And the nobleman cried, "There is one."

Then he served the next one in the same manner, crying, "There is the second." So he went to the next and the next and full down the line, passing all the twelve, giving each a sound whack and crying out

129

their number. He reached the last man and hit him extra hard, crying, "Here is the twelfth one."

The men of Gotham rubbed their shoulders, but there was gladness on their faces, for now they knew that they were all present.

"God's blessing on your heart," they all cried, "for having found our neighbor," and they went off merrily.

Said the nobleman to Jack:

"Certes these men have not head enough to fool the king of the realm. Methinks here are the fools of fools for which you have been searching."

But Jack grumbled, for he was still in doubt. And truly a doubter sees many ghosts.

The true lord of the merry men of Gotham

LISTEN, the last of the tales!

Cutting Tom, renowned for his bravery and merry

19

jests, grew up in Nottingham. Finding the ways of Gotham to his liking, he went to live there, and in quick time he became a true citizen of the town. He was ever merry, acted wise or otherwise, always found new ways to do old things, and didn't mind what the rest of the world said about it.

Now, one day Jack of Dover, a-riding with the justice of the peace, a very proud man, met Cutting Tom, who also was a-riding on a horse. They met in a very narrow lane, each going the opposite way.

Now, Cutting Tom, like the rest of the people of Gotham, did not like Jack, nor the justice of the peace, either. Prompted by deviltry, he forced the proud fellows, who would have the whole road, against the wall and almost tumbled the justice off his horse. This put both into a rage.

Shouted the justice of the peace:

"Varlet! Gallows bird! Didn't you see who was coming your way? I've a good mind to see you dangling for that. Who are you, anyway, you witless ape, who cannot step aside when you see your betters on the road?"

"I am a man, just as you two are," Cutting Tom replied.

"Whom do you serve, to speak to me in this manner?" cried the justice.

"Why, I serve none other than God, Master Justice," quoth Tom.

"Serve God!" cried the justice. "Do you mock me? Can't you answer straight like a man? Marry, we'll see how you'll answer after you've cooled your heels in prison. Ho, there, soldier!" This, to the fellow who followed him. "Carry the knave to prison. I'll teach him how to answer directly. Serves God! There's an answer for you, Master Jack. These Gotham fools think they can do any deed without punishment."

"Aye, that is so," replied Jack of Dover.

To jail Cutting Tom was led, and there he lay the whole night. On the morrow he was brought once

133

again before the justice of the peace. Jack of Dover was by his side.

"Tell me, fellow, whom do you serve now? Perhaps after cooling your hot head in prison you can give a more direct reply."

"No better reply than yesterday can I have for you today," answered Cutting Tom. "I still serve God."

"But," said the justice, "don't you serve some lord of a castle or a franklin?"

"I do indeed serve my President of York."

"Oddsblood, knave, why didn't you say so the first time? I'd never have put you in prison for the night."

"Marry," quoth Cutting Tom, "because I thought you loved our Lord God more than the lord of the town. Now I see that you'll set me free for the sake of the lord of the town and not for the sake of the Lord in Heaven. Ha, Master Justice, that's a fine tale!"

"You speak like a knave of Gotham, from which fools come."

"Nay, Master Justice," Cutting Tom quickly replied, "I come from Gotham, to which fools often come."

There was a great laugh from the crowd, and the justice let Tom free.

Jack went his way much abashed, mumbling into his beard he'd had enough of the fools of Gotham and some other words which no one could understand.

But, whatever words he said, it mattered little to the men of Gotham, for they were merry, with little care as to what crabbed folk thought of them. Therein they acted like many famous wise men in the world. And therefore, to this very day, there are many who say that the deeds of the merry men of Gotham were more wise than otherwise.

As for Jack of Dover, he went on a-roaming along the highways and cities, seeking the fool of fools, till one day, when he sat in a grand learned company, one wise man turned to him and said:

135

"Marry, I wonder if you, Jack, are not the veriest fool in England for spending your golden time seeking such a fool when you can spend those precious hours to a better purpose."

And all there present agreed with him, and so do you and I.

Thus end here
The tales of the Wise Men of Gotham
and of
Jack of Dover
of
merry England

Three wise men of Gotham
Went to sea in a bowl,
And if the bowl had been stronger,
My tale would have been longer.

136

A little history of
the Gotham
folk tales

THE tales of the Merry Men of Gotham, sunned, seasoned, and mellowed by the centuries, have such an interesting history that I am certain you would like to know a little of it.

But before telling you the sparkling life of these stories for near three hundred years, I want to tell you how I set them down for you to read.

Stories, to me, are the glowing decorations of the hours of daily life. They brighten them up joyfully, just as starry lights a Christmas tree. When I meet exciting, near-forgotten tales that have not been told, I want to tell them at once to all the world.

I have known these tales since I could understand sentences. One day I read what Mr. Stapleton, the great English scholar, wrote about fifty years ago of these Gotham tales. Said he: "The once very popular story (of Gotham) is now quite a thing of the past. It has passed away into oblivion. . . . Probably it was the longest lived as well as the widest read of all the English Jest books, for it appears to have run fully three centuries from its earliest to its latest printing. . . . There seems to be no reason why . . .

138

a selection of these tales should not be utilized for children's books in the present day. Few subjects would be better suited for the purpose than, say, the first ten tales of Gotham. We shall confidently await this hint being taken up and hope thus to see the ancient stories and jests once more revived."

I fully agree with the late Mr. Stapleton. These stories, told to me when I was knee high, had given me exciting pleasure. As the march of years went on, I often wondered why they were not reprinted for all to enjoy. Finally, it occurred to me that perhaps they were not presented the way we like stories today, for they seemed to be just small anecdotes.

So I took these jests and anecdotes, blowing about the lands like spring pollens for many hundred years under such titles as *Tales of Gotham, Merry Tales of the Mad Men of Gotham,* and others, and set them down in my own words, in my own form, and my own way—in story form for you to read.

In the world's history of stories, stories have

139

changed with the storyteller, and ever since the Gotham stories began they have changed according to the place where they were told and who told them.

Even as early as about 1662, Master Fuller, a learned gentleman and writer said: "An hundred fopperies are feigned and fathered on the town-folk of Gotham, a village in this country."

I did not put in any of the stories which are not held to be true Gotham salt. In none of the stories have I changed the jest or idea; the difference is mainly in the telling, in creating a little lively interest. There is now a slight continuity through the tales, a simple thread which in a way gives them a beginning, a middle, and an end. Now and then, as in the tale "Grazing on the Roof," I combined several tales to fit this continuity.

In order to do this, I have added a few of the stories of the legendary Jack of Dover, who, in tales told and written, roamed the land in quest of the greatest fool in England. Surely in this quest he must have come many times to Gotham.

Now, Jack of Dover mingled not only with earthy folk but with gaping nobles as well, and so, it is fair to assume, he belonged, if not completely, at least in large part, to the king's party rather than to that of the common folk. For that reason, in the story, he sides with King John and not with the men of Gotham.

Believe me, not for a moment did I think I could improve on the robust, rollicking humor of the original jests and anecdotes. But even the fine scholar, Mr. Stapleton, put at the end of his bright, scholarly book, *All about the Merry Tales of Gotham,* his own, more modern version of these stories.

If you would like to read the jests and anecdotes as they appeared in the first printing, you will find them in the before-mentioned book by Mr. Stapleton. There they appear in a modernized version of the 1630 edition.

141

You will also find them in *Merry Tales of the Mad Men of Gotham,* edited by W. Carew Hazlitt. In that book they are put down exactly as they were in the 1630 edition.

They are also in the modern edition of James O. Halliwell, under the title of *The Merry Tales of the Wise Men of Gotham.*

The Jack of Dover tales can be found complete in *Jack of Dover's Quest of Inquirie,* edited by W. Carew Hazlitt.

No one knows when or even where these stories began. Either they just happened here and there, or the seeds were scattered through the lands by some nimble-minded folk traveling far and wide and bore fruit wherever they fell. You will find the same kind of stories in almost every country in the world—in Asia and in Africa, in France and in Italy, in ancient Greece, in ancient Egypt, and among the Jews in the days of the Bible.

Take such a story as fishing for the image of the moon that looks like a moving yellow cheese in the silent water. That story has been told in almost every living land by folk in search of a happy minute of laughter.

The same is true of the story of drowning the eel, or of counting the twelve men to make certain all are there. There is a particularly delightful, funny, folksy version of that tale in India.

These stories are like rays of an enormous golden sun, shedding happy, warming laughter wherever they shine.

Now, it has always been a very human habit, in every land, to plant such stories around a particular town or people. The Greeks made fun of Sidonians, the Swiss laughed at the simpletons of Belmont. The Persian Arabs ha-ha'd at the silly folk in Hums, and New York City people poke fun at the folk in Brooklyn. The Negro North African tribes think the people of Beni-Jennad are very silly, and Hollanders

143

burst with laughter at the folk of Kampan. In Belgium there are funny tales about the Dinant citizens, and in France about Les Anes de Beaune. This custom snakes its way throughout all the world and is probably a simple way for people to place their own follies on other men's doorsteps.

There really was, and still is, in England a peaceful, sun-bright village called Gotham. It is near Nottingham, not very far from Sherwood Forest, famous for Robin Hood and his hard, merry-living men.

If you go to Gotham, folk there will show you the Cuckoo Bush on Court Hill, where the men of Gotham tried to keep that bird to sing for them the whole year 'round. They will show you Cheese Hill, where the yellow cheeses rolled down through the green grass. And they will show you King John's Mound, where the wise men of Gotham fooled King John just as you have read in the story.

There also was a legendary Jack of Dover in tales and print who runs in and out of the stories. Many

144

an adventure is told of his attempt to find the fool of fools in England. Some of them are so amusing that I could not help but put them into this book.

Just why the tales were tacked on Gotham town rather than London or any other town is hidden in the years gone by. Perhaps it was done because Gotham in the old Anglo-Saxon meant goats' town, and the goat, from the most ancient days, was always considered a silly animal.

Perhaps it was a section of England where many unusual things happened. Sherwood Forest, right nearby, was full of stories about famous Robin Hood and his adventures. Or perhaps because some gossipy fellow was outwitted by Gotham folk at some time.

Whatever the cause, we find that these comic stories were mostly connected with Gotham. They are mentioned even in the reign of Henry VI in a collection of miracle plays, as religious plays were then called. That was around 1425.

The fame of the name of Gotham spread through

145

all the world—even to America, where New York City is called Gotham and New Yorkers are called Gothamites because they are so "smart" in their behavior.

There were endless Gotham stories, anecdotes, and jests—many, many more than ever appeared in the printed book we know.

In the first printing of them we have, it states in one tale: "In old time, when these aforesaid jests, as men of the country reported, and such fantastical matters were done at Gotham, which I cannot tell half."

Quite often, stories of other localities were pinned on the folk of Gotham. In the earliest printed book of them, which contains only twenty of the tales, near half of them were not really Gotham drolleries.

Here are the sources, the toothy kernels around which I built the stories of this book:

Story 1 is my own introduction.

Stories 3, 4, 6, 8, 11, 12, 14, 15, 17, and 18 are original accredited Gotham tales.

146

Stories 2, 7, 9, and 13 are traditional Gotham tales not found in the regular collections, but they can be found scattered in Stapleton's book, and also in *The Book of Noodles,* by W. A. Clouston, and other works dealing with ancient comic stories.

Stories 5, 10, 16, and 19 are *Jack of Dover's Quest of Inquirie* tales.

The earliest printed version mentioned is around 1556-1566. It was *Merrie Tales of the Mad Men of Gotham,* gathered together by A. B. Phisike Doctour. A. B. is supposed to stand for Andrew Borde, a Carthusian friar, a traveler, a scholar, and a physician.

The earliest version we have is the one printed in 1630 with the same title. There were many printings of the stories thenafter in the same form. None of the spoken stories were added to later printings, nor were those taken away which really were not true Gotham tales.

As time went along, the stories lost their popularity except among students and scholars.

147

The verses throughout the book are old rhymes common in different parts of England for centuries.

It is interesting to note that throughout the years when they were popular, people often could not make up their minds whether the Gothamites really were silly or just acted silly to gain their ends. Some called them Merry Men, some Wise Men, some Silly Men, and some even Mad Men. There were arguments in homes and inns in the land as to whether they acted silly because they were silly or acted silly because they were wise and found they could get what they wanted easier that way.

Now, you know, most people in the world have a little bit of silliness and a little bit of wisdom in them, and that is good, for the two combined often bring good laughter. Surely a town of people that could outwit a king of the realm by acting silly would try the same on other folk. The men of Gotham in the stories had learned that the wisdom of life is to be pleased with little, and that a good laugh is worth more than shining silver.

148

An old writer said: "Gotham doth breed as wise people as any which laugh at their simplicity."

Again, there is an old proverb: "As wise as the men of Gotham," which can be taken in two ways. There was also an old saying: "More fools pass through Gotham than remain in it."

One day a stranger passed a boy working in a brown field in Gotham and said: "Is this the Gotham that fools come from?"

"No, sir," said the boy, "this is the Gotham that fools come to."

Mr. Stapleton, the eminent scholar and student of the Gotham tales, also held "that it was likely as not that whosoever first set the tales on foot was aggrieved because some Gothamite had been clever for him, not foolish."

I take it that the little, warmhearted village had its proper share of gangling silly men and understanding wise men, as most villages in the world have. And when the wise ones in the village saw that the behavior of the silly ones was really for the best and brought luck and laughter, the finest medicine in the world for men's ills—when they saw that here was "folly in wisdom hatched," they probably decided to continue the pleasant game that brought no harm to anyone and pleasure and profit to themselves.

It is in that spirit that I put down these tales—the tales of the Merry, Silly, Wise, Mad Men of Gotham and of Jack of Dover, who was a little like the men of Gotham. May they give you the same pleasure they gave the folk of green England for full three hundred years or maybe more.

M. Jagendorf
Old Cole Farm, Putnam County
New York

150